P9-DJA-305

Brown County Public Library
205 Locust Lane / PO Box 8
Nashville, IN 47448

Ph. 812-988-2850 Fax 812-988-8119

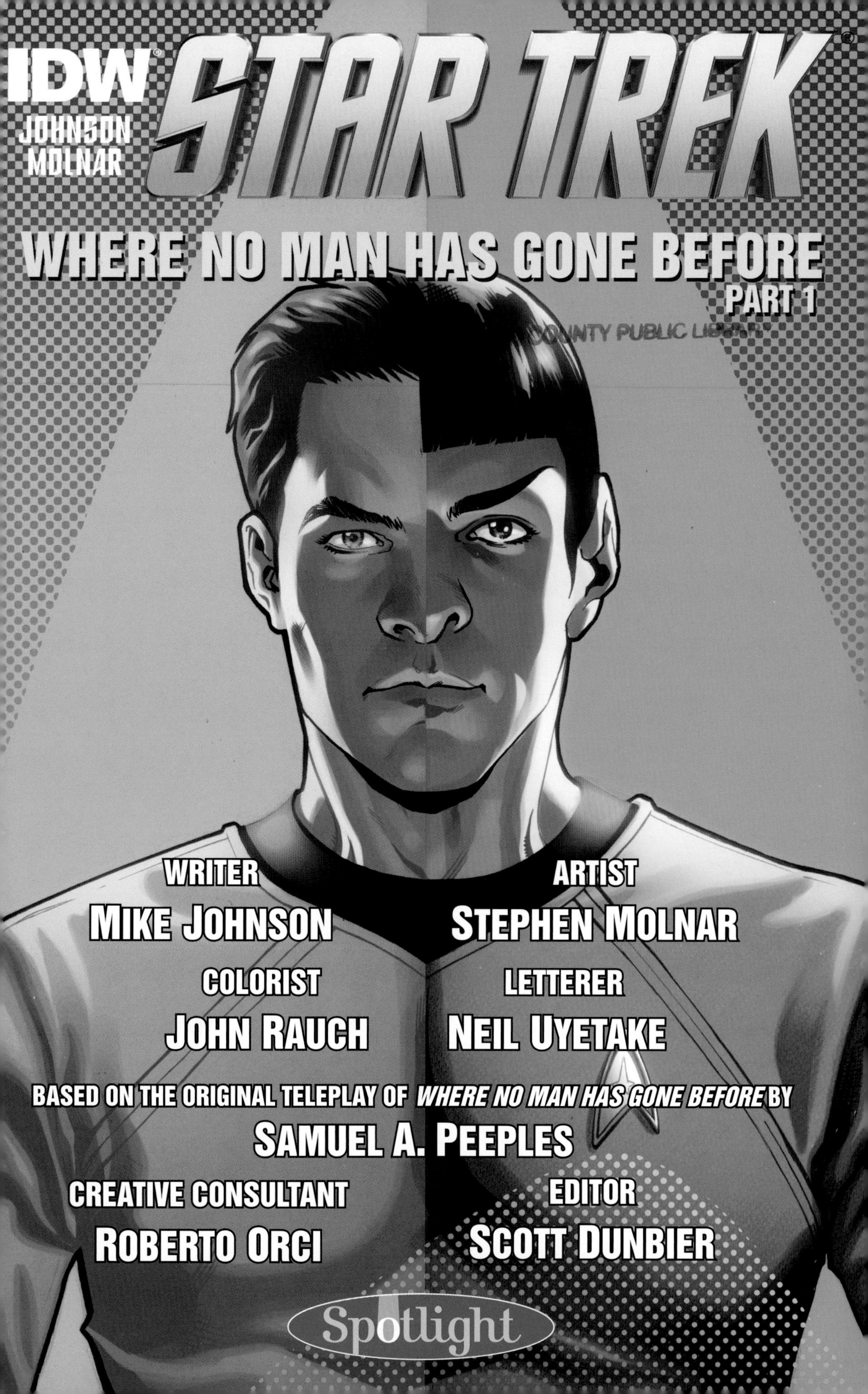
IDW
JOHNSON
MOLNAR
STAR TREK
WHERE NO MAN HAS GONE BEFORE
PART 1
WRITER
MIKE JOHNSON
ARTIST
STEPHEN MOLNAR
COLORIST
JOHN RAUCH
LETTERER
NEIL UYETAKE
BASED ON THE ORIGINAL TELEPLAY OF *WHERE NO MAN HAS GONE BEFORE* BY
SAMUEL A. PEEPLES
CREATIVE CONSULTANT
ROBERTO ORCI
EDITOR
SCOTT DUNBIER
Spotlight

Visit us at www.abdopublishing.com

Reinforced library bound editions published in 2014 by Spotlight, a division of the ABDO Group, PO Box 398166, Minneapolis, MN 55439. Spotlight produces high-quality reinforced library bound editions for schools and libraries. Published by agreement with IDW.

Printed in the United States of America, North Mankato, Minnesota.
042013
092013
♻ This book contains at least 10% recycled material.

STAR TREK created by Gene Roddenberry.
Special thanks to Risa Kessler and John Van Citters of CBS Consumer Products for their invaluable assistance.

STAR TREK: Where No Man Has Gone Before: Part 1. ® & © 2011 CBS Studios Inc. *STAR TREK* and related marks and trademarks of CBS Studios Inc. © 2011 Paramount Pictures Corporation. All Rights Reserved. IDW Publishing authorized user. © 2011 Idea and Design Works, LLC. IDW Publishing, a division of Idea and Design Works, LLC. Any similarites to persons living or dead are purely coincidental. With the exception of artwork used for review purposes, none of the contents of this publication may be reprinted without the permission of Idea and Design Works, LLC.

Library of Congress Cataloging-in-Publication Data

Johnson, Mike.
  Where no man has gone before / story by Mike Johnson ; art by Stephen Molnar.
      volumes cm. -- (Star Trek)
   ISBN 978-1-61479-161-4 (part 1) -- ISBN 978-1-61479-162-1 (part 2)
 1. Graphic novels. I. Molnar, Stephen, illustrator. II. Title.
 PZ7.7.J6417Whe 2014
 741.5'973--dc23
                            2013004267

All Spotlight books are reinforced library bindings
and manufactured in the United States of America.

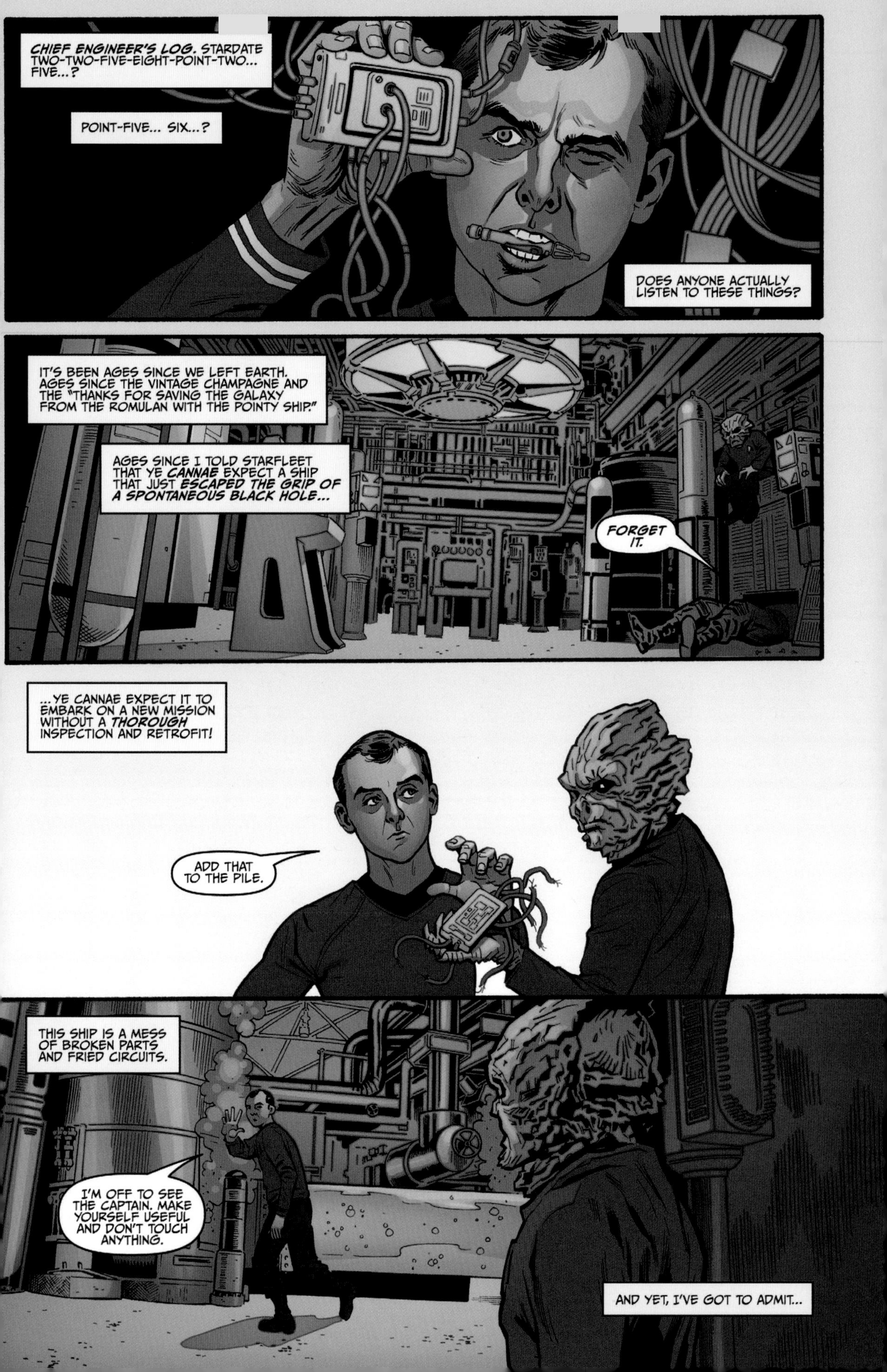
CHIEF ENGINEER'S LOG. STARDATE TWO-TWO-FIVE-EIGHT-POINT-TWO... FIVE...?
POINT-FIVE... SIX...?
DOES ANYONE ACTUALLY LISTEN TO THESE THINGS?
IT'S BEEN AGES SINCE WE LEFT EARTH. AGES SINCE THE VINTAGE CHAMPAGNE AND THE "THANKS FOR SAVING THE GALAXY FROM THE ROMULAN WITH THE POINTY SHIP."
AGES SINCE I TOLD STARFLEET THAT YE CANNAE EXPECT A SHIP THAT JUST ESCAPED THE GRIP OF A SPONTANEOUS BLACK HOLE...
FORGET IT.
...YE CANNAE EXPECT IT TO EMBARK ON A NEW MISSION WITHOUT A THOROUGH INSPECTION AND RETROFIT!
ADD THAT TO THE PILE.
THIS SHIP IS A MESS OF BROKEN PARTS AND FRIED CIRCUITS.
I'M OFF TO SEE THE CAPTAIN. MAKE YOURSELF USEFUL AND DON'T TOUCH ANYTHING.
AND YET, I'VE GOT TO ADMIT...

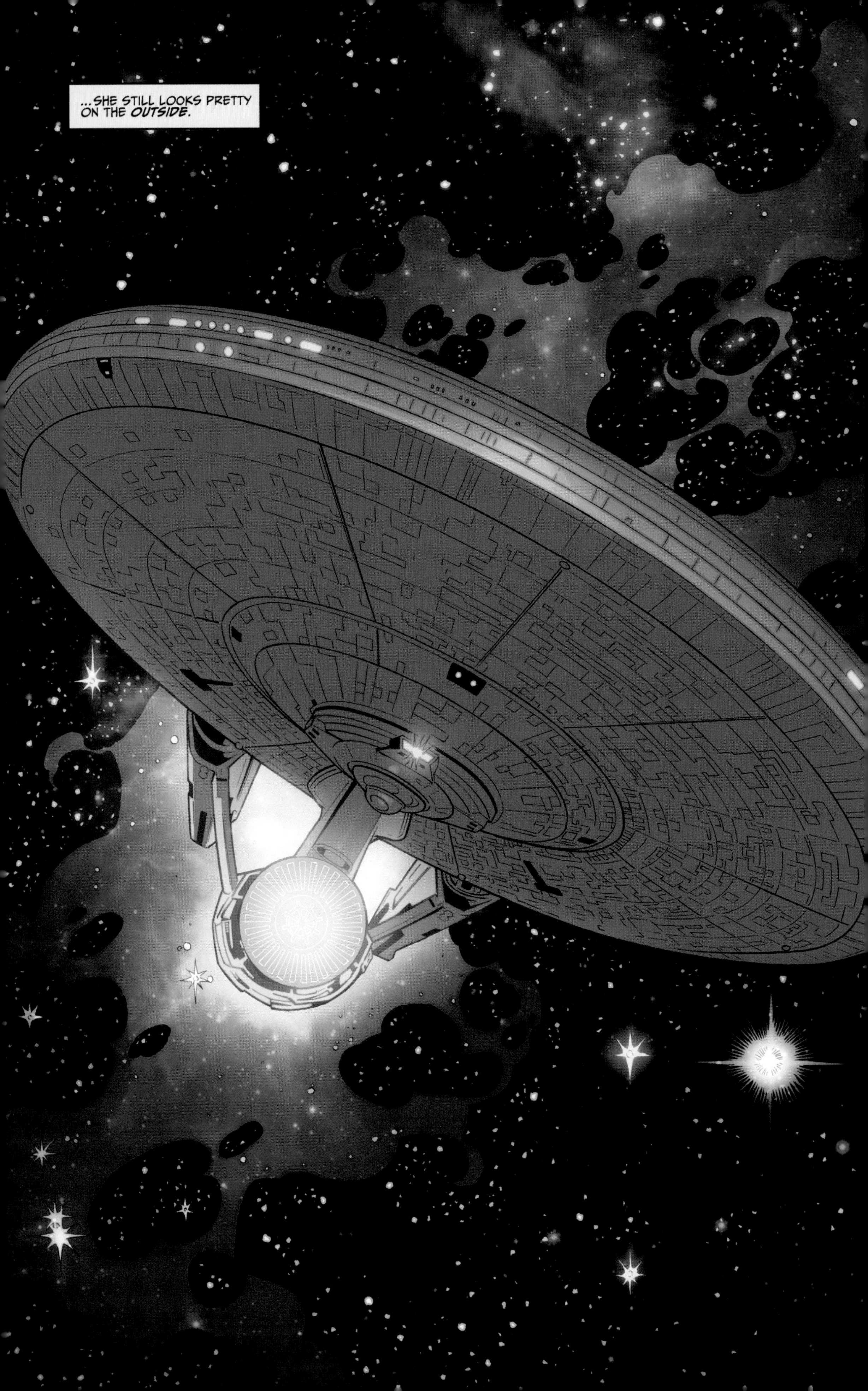
...SHE STILL LOOKS PRETTY ON THE *OUTSIDE*.

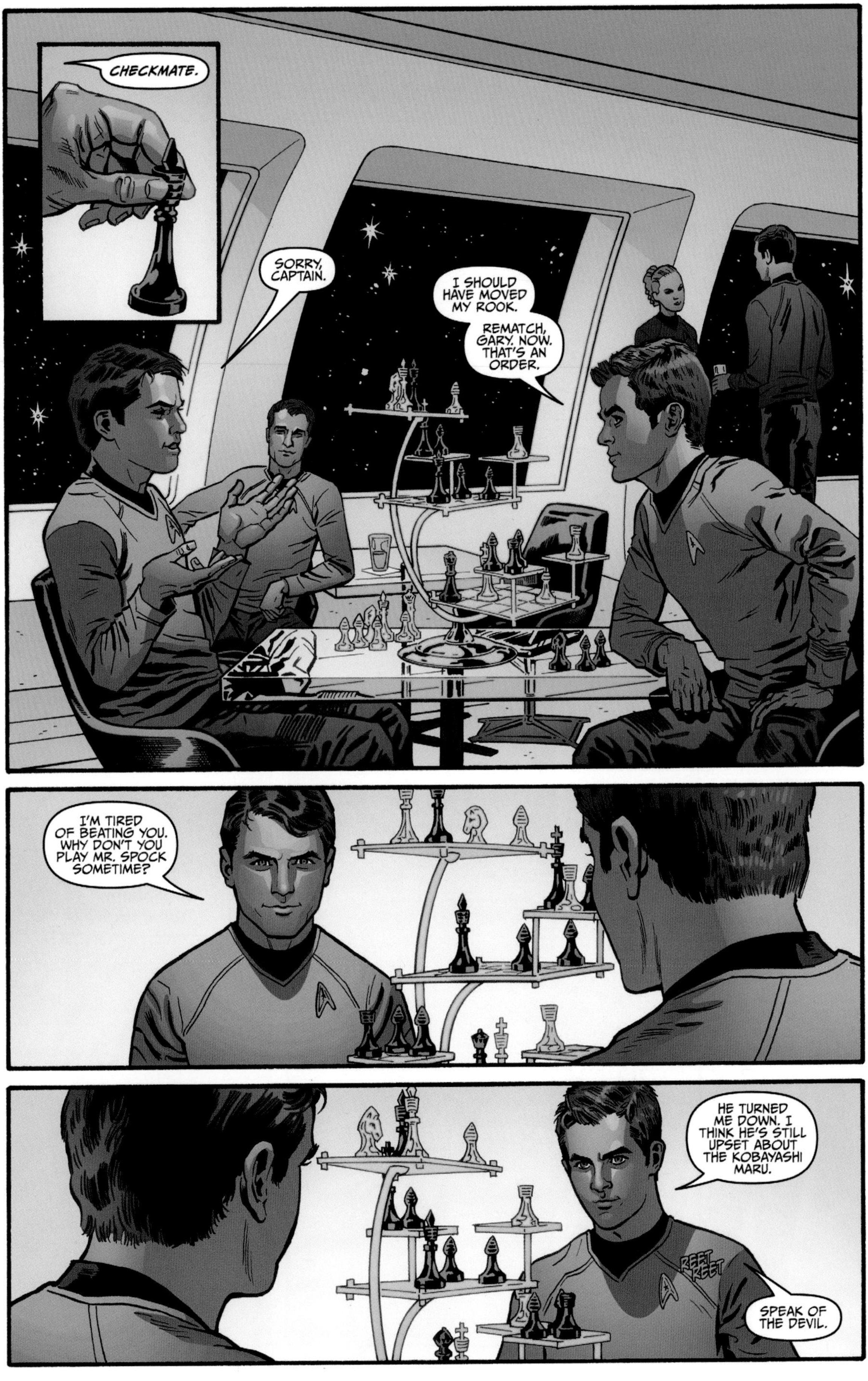
CHECKMATE.
SORRY, CAPTAIN.
I SHOULD HAVE MOVED MY ROOK.
REMATCH, GARY. NOW. THAT'S AN ORDER.
I'M TIRED OF BEATING YOU. WHY DON'T YOU PLAY MR. SPOCK SOMETIME?
HE TURNED ME DOWN. I THINK HE'S STILL UPSET ABOUT THE KOBAYASHI MARU.
REET REET
SPEAK OF THE DEVIL.

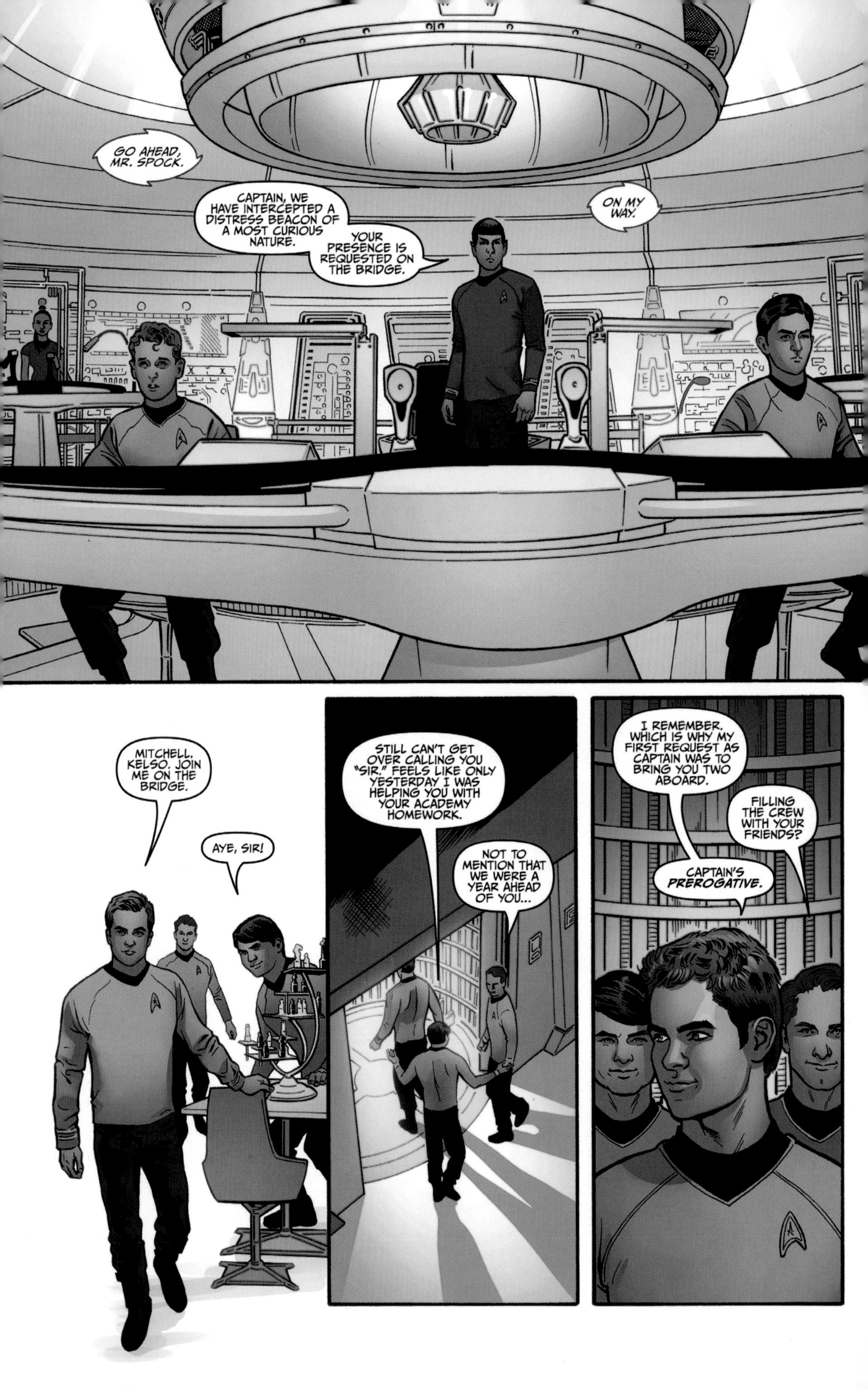
GO AHEAD, MR. SPOCK.
CAPTAIN, WE HAVE INTERCEPTED A DISTRESS BEACON OF A MOST CURIOUS NATURE.
YOUR PRESENCE IS REQUESTED ON THE BRIDGE.
ON MY WAY.
MITCHELL, KELSO. JOIN ME ON THE BRIDGE.
AYE, SIR!
STILL CAN'T GET OVER CALLING YOU "SIR." FEELS LIKE ONLY YESTERDAY I WAS HELPING YOU WITH YOUR ACADEMY HOMEWORK.
NOT TO MENTION THAT WE WERE A YEAR AHEAD OF YOU...
I REMEMBER. WHICH IS WHY MY FIRST REQUEST AS CAPTAIN WAS TO BRING YOU TWO ABOARD.
FILLING THE CREW WITH YOUR FRIENDS?
CAPTAIN'S *PREROGATIVE.*

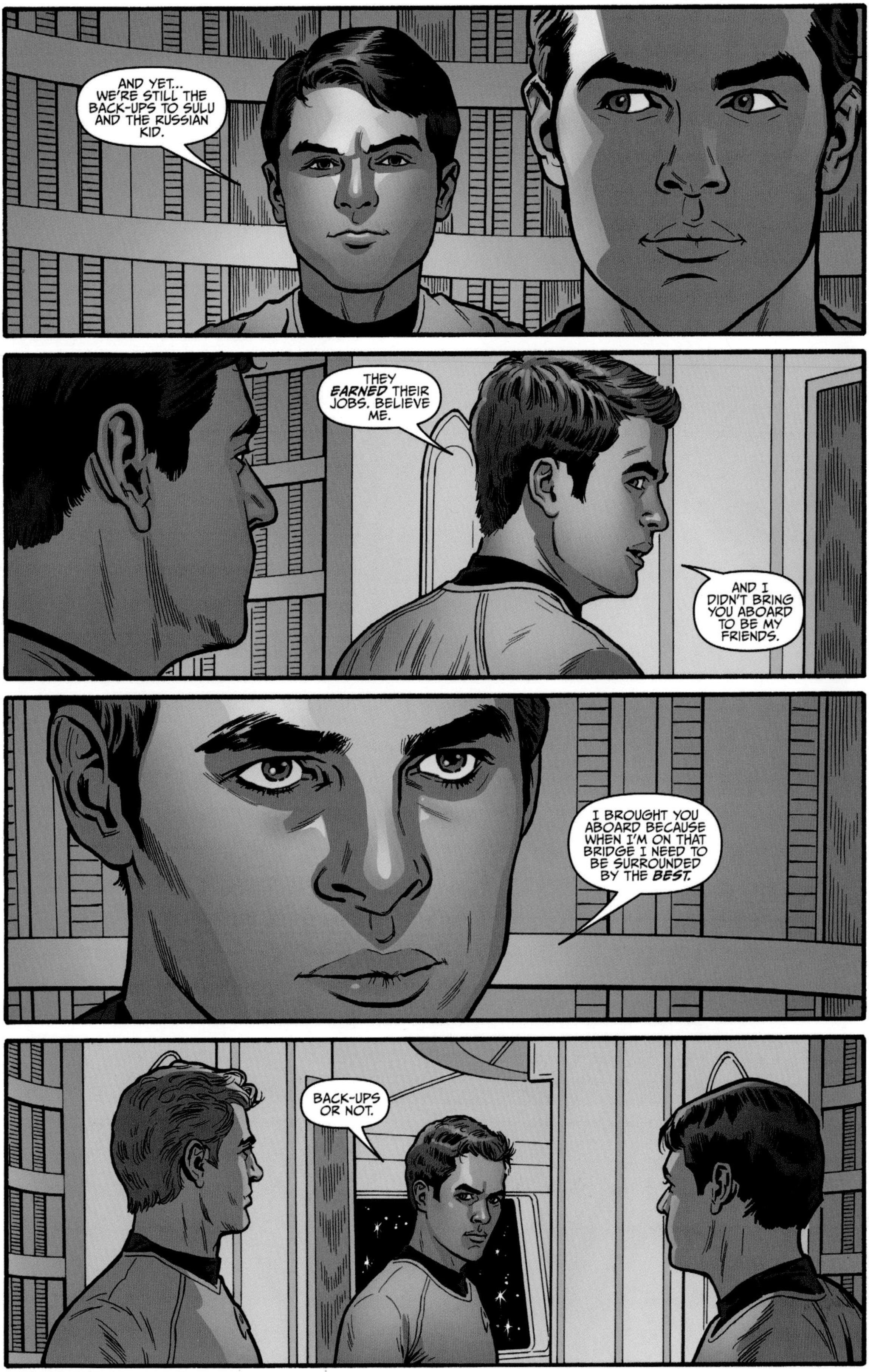
AND YET... WE'RE STILL THE BACK-UPS TO SULU AND THE RUSSIAN KID.
THEY *EARNED* THEIR JOBS. BELIEVE ME.
AND I DIDN'T BRING YOU ABOARD TO BE MY FRIENDS.
I BROUGHT YOU ABOARD BECAUSE WHEN I'M ON THAT BRIDGE I NEED TO BE SURROUNDED BY THE *BEST*.
BACK-UPS OR NOT.

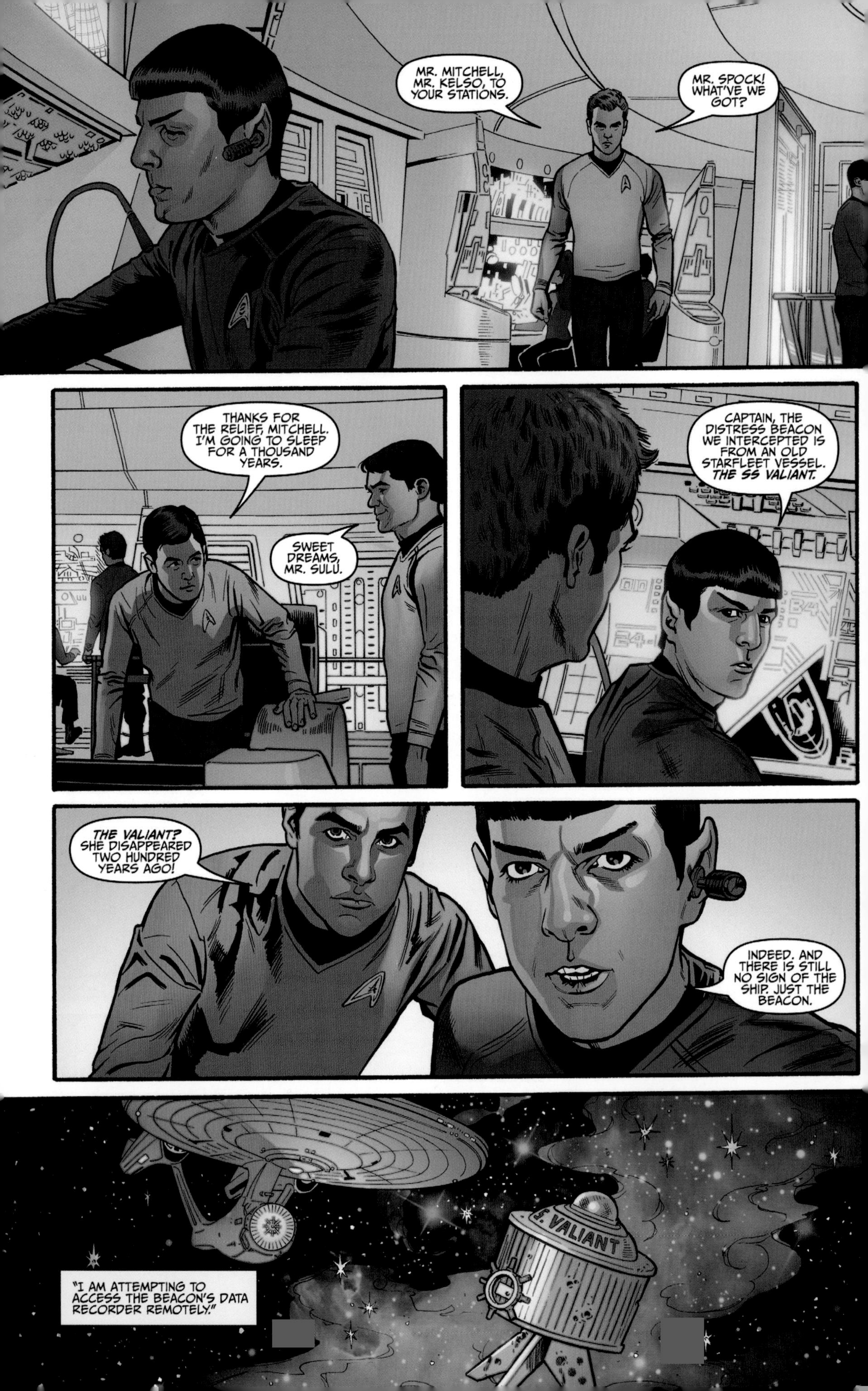
MR. MITCHELL, MR. KELSO, TO YOUR STATIONS.
MR. SPOCK! WHAT'VE WE GOT?
THANKS FOR THE RELIEF, MITCHELL. I'M GOING TO SLEEP FOR A THOUSAND YEARS.
SWEET DREAMS, MR. SULU.
CAPTAIN, THE DISTRESS BEACON WE INTERCEPTED IS FROM AN OLD STARFLEET VESSEL. THE SS VALIANT.
THE VALIANT? SHE DISAPPEARED TWO HUNDRED YEARS AGO!
INDEED. AND THERE IS STILL NO SIGN OF THE SHIP. JUST THE BEACON.
S. VALIANT
"I AM ATTEMPTING TO ACCESS THE BEACON'S DATA RECORDER REMOTELY."

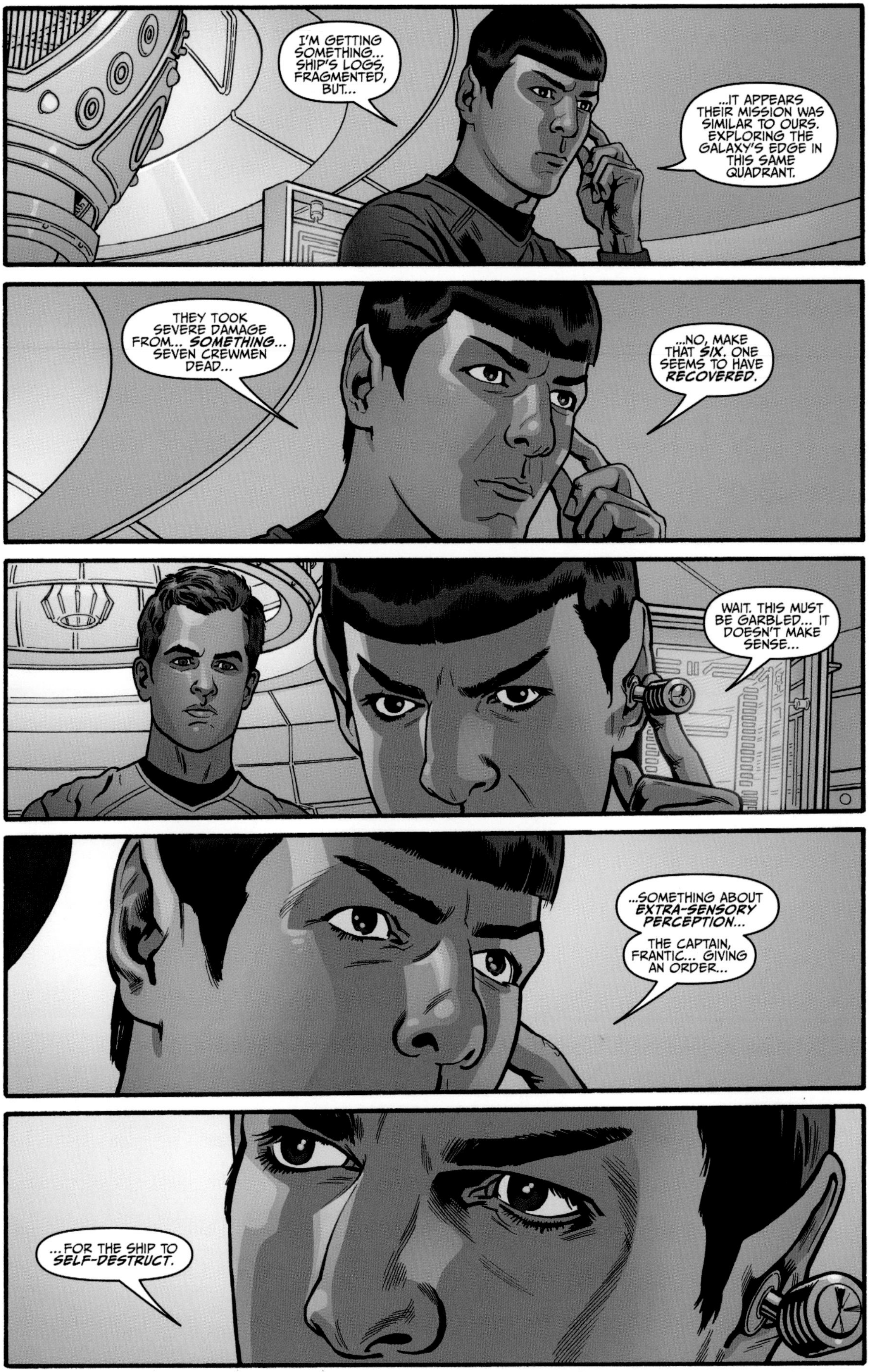
I'M GETTING SOMETHING... SHIP'S LOGS, FRAGMENTED, BUT...
...IT APPEARS THEIR MISSION WAS SIMILAR TO OURS. EXPLORING THE GALAXY'S EDGE IN THIS SAME QUADRANT.
THEY TOOK SEVERE DAMAGE FROM... SOMETHING... SEVEN CREWMEN DEAD...
...NO, MAKE THAT SIX. ONE SEEMS TO HAVE RECOVERED.
WAIT. THIS MUST BE GARBLED... IT DOESN'T MAKE SENSE...
...SOMETHING ABOUT EXTRA-SENSORY PERCEPTION...
THE CAPTAIN, FRANTIC... GIVING AN ORDER...
...FOR THE SHIP TO SELF-DESTRUCT.

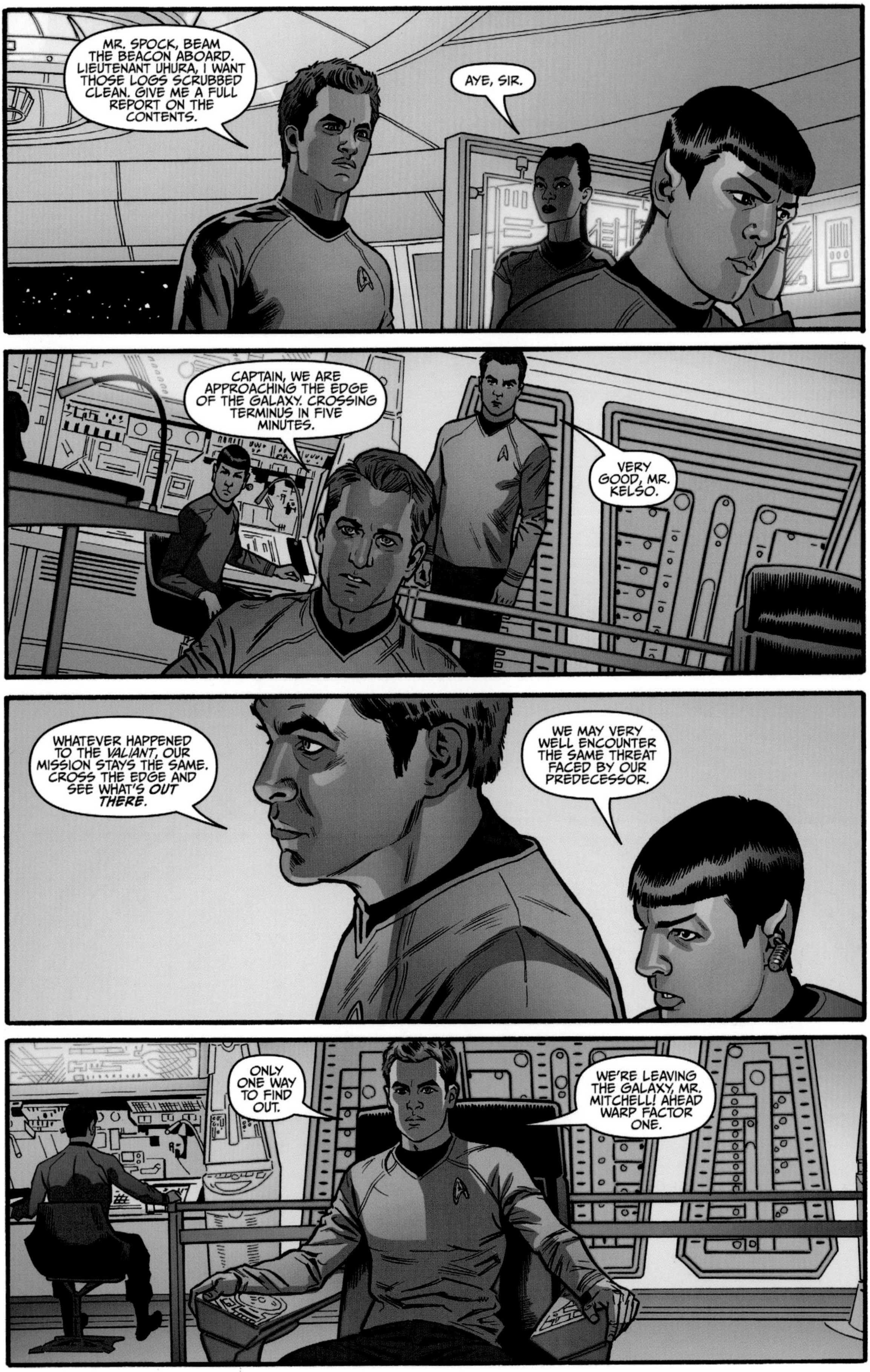
MR. SPOCK, BEAM THE BEACON ABOARD. LIEUTENANT UHURA, I WANT THOSE LOGS SCRUBBED CLEAN. GIVE ME A FULL REPORT ON THE CONTENTS.
AYE, SIR.
CAPTAIN, WE ARE APPROACHING THE EDGE OF THE GALAXY. CROSSING TERMINUS IN FIVE MINUTES.
VERY GOOD, MR. KELSO.
WHATEVER HAPPENED TO THE *VALIANT*, OUR MISSION STAYS THE SAME. CROSS THE EDGE AND SEE WHAT'S ***OUT THERE***.
WE MAY VERY WELL ENCOUNTER THE SAME THREAT FACED BY OUR PREDECESSOR.
ONLY ONE WAY TO FIND OUT.
WE'RE LEAVING THE GALAXY, MR. MITCHELL! AHEAD WARP FACTOR ONE.

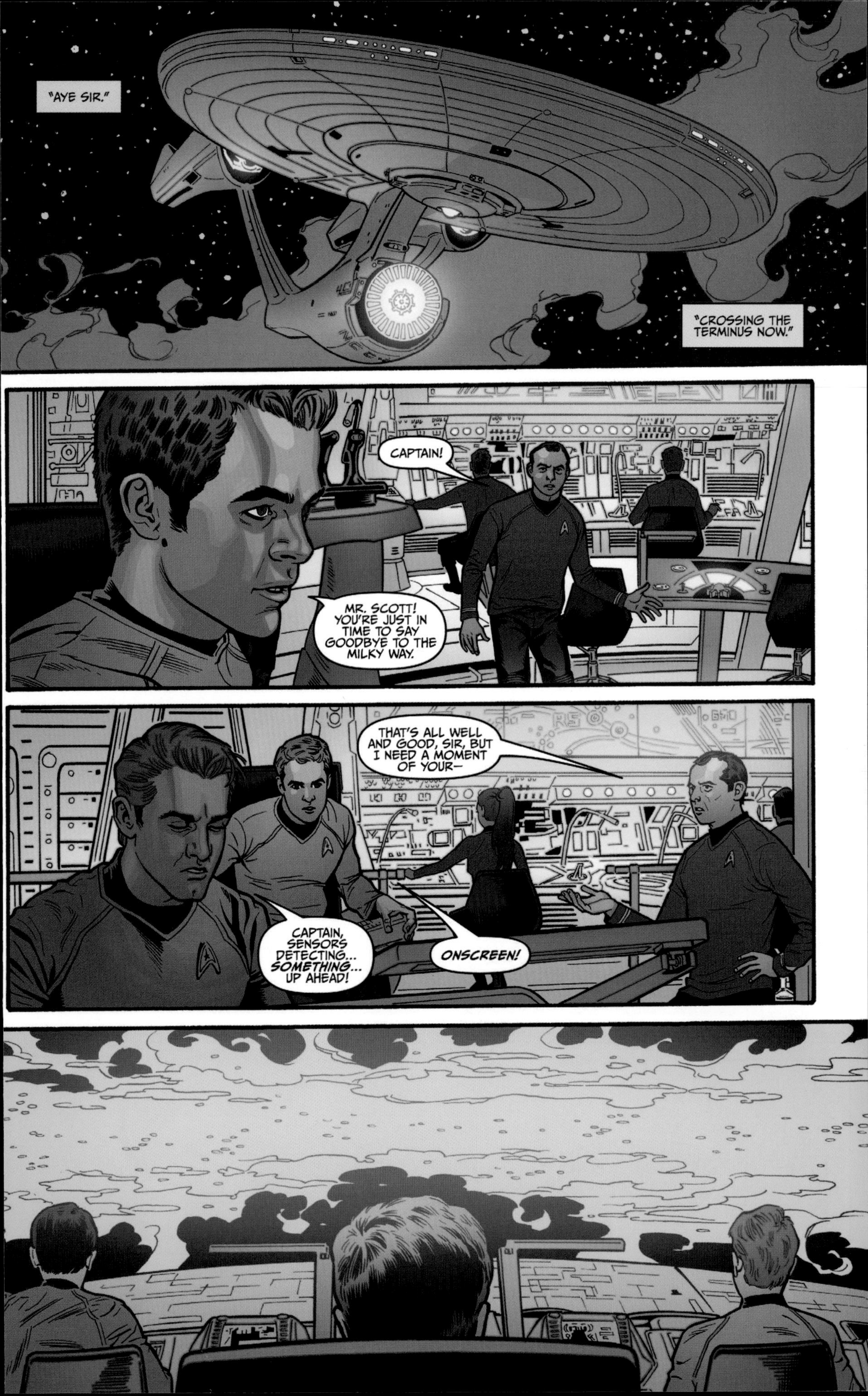
"AYE SIR."
"CROSSING THE TERMINUS NOW."
CAPTAIN!
MR. SCOTT! YOU'RE JUST IN TIME TO SAY GOODBYE TO THE MILKY WAY.
THAT'S ALL WELL AND GOOD, SIR, BUT I NEED A MOMENT OF YOUR—
CAPTAIN, SENSORS DETECTING... SOMETHING... UP AHEAD!
ONSCREEN!

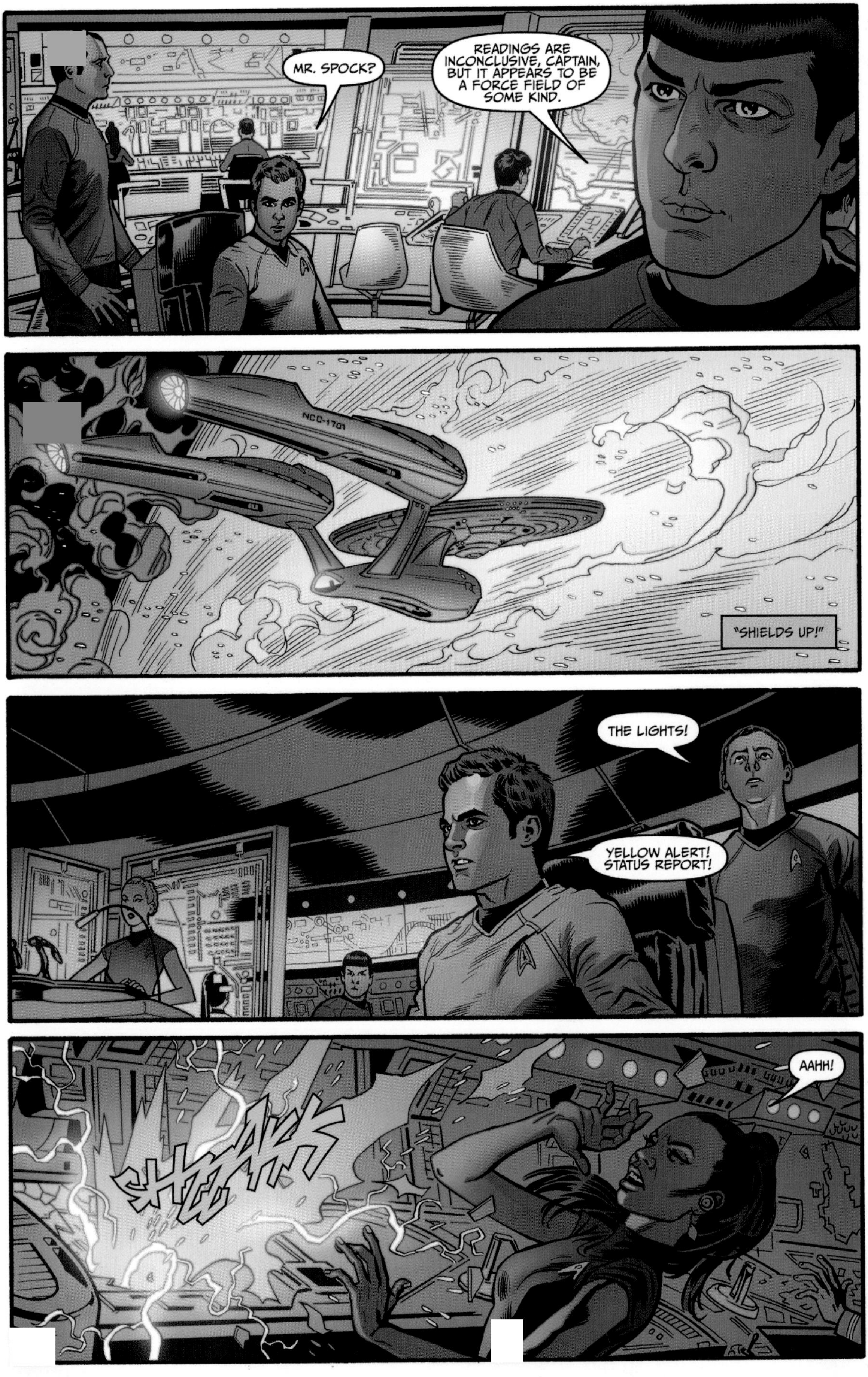
MR. SPOCK?
READINGS ARE INCONCLUSIVE, CAPTAIN, BUT IT APPEARS TO BE A FORCE FIELD OF SOME KIND.
NCC-1701
"SHIELDS UP!"
THE LIGHTS!
YELLOW ALERT! STATUS REPORT!
AAHH!

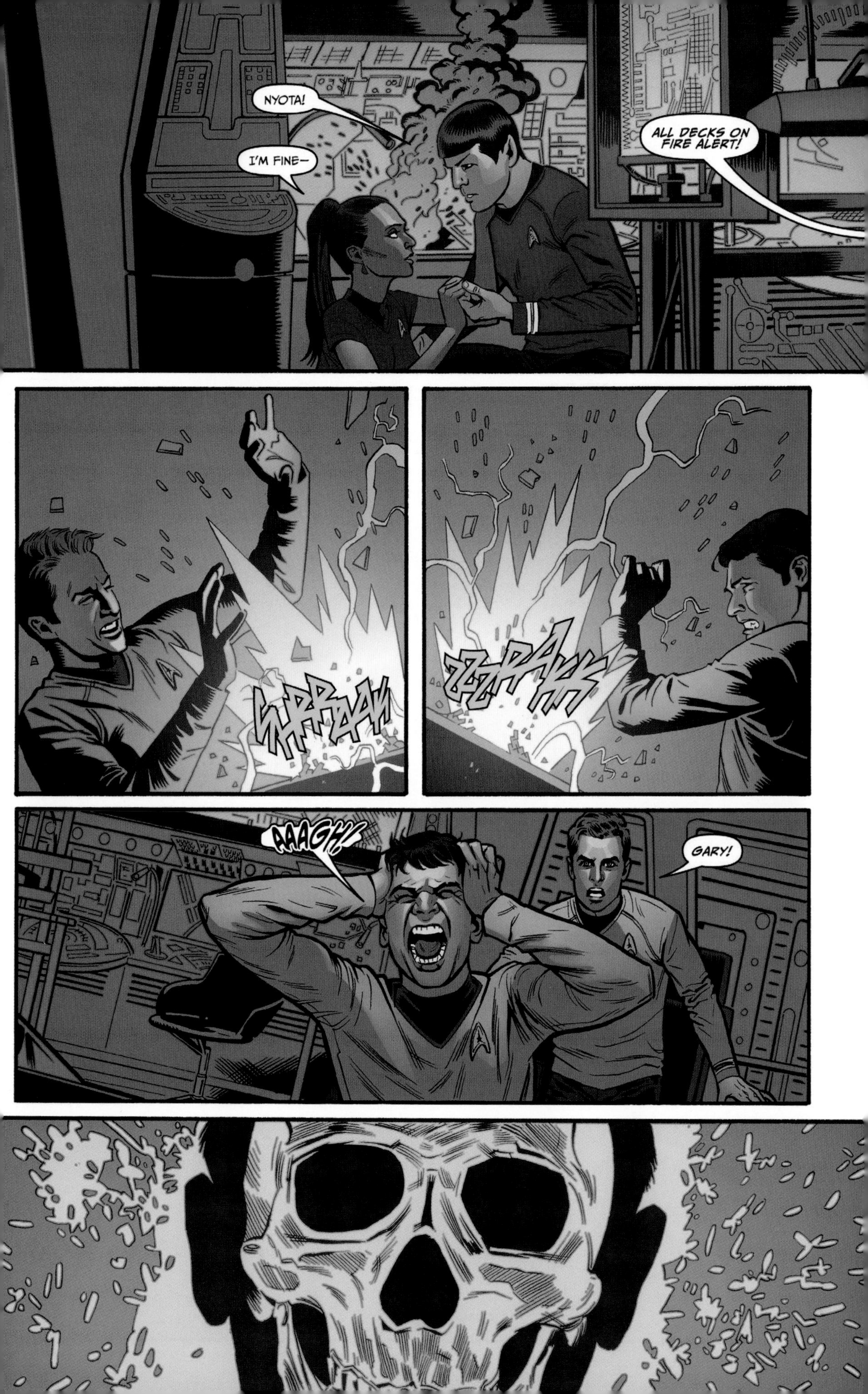
NYOTA!
I'M FINE—
ALL DECKS ON FIRE ALERT!
AAAGH!
GARY!

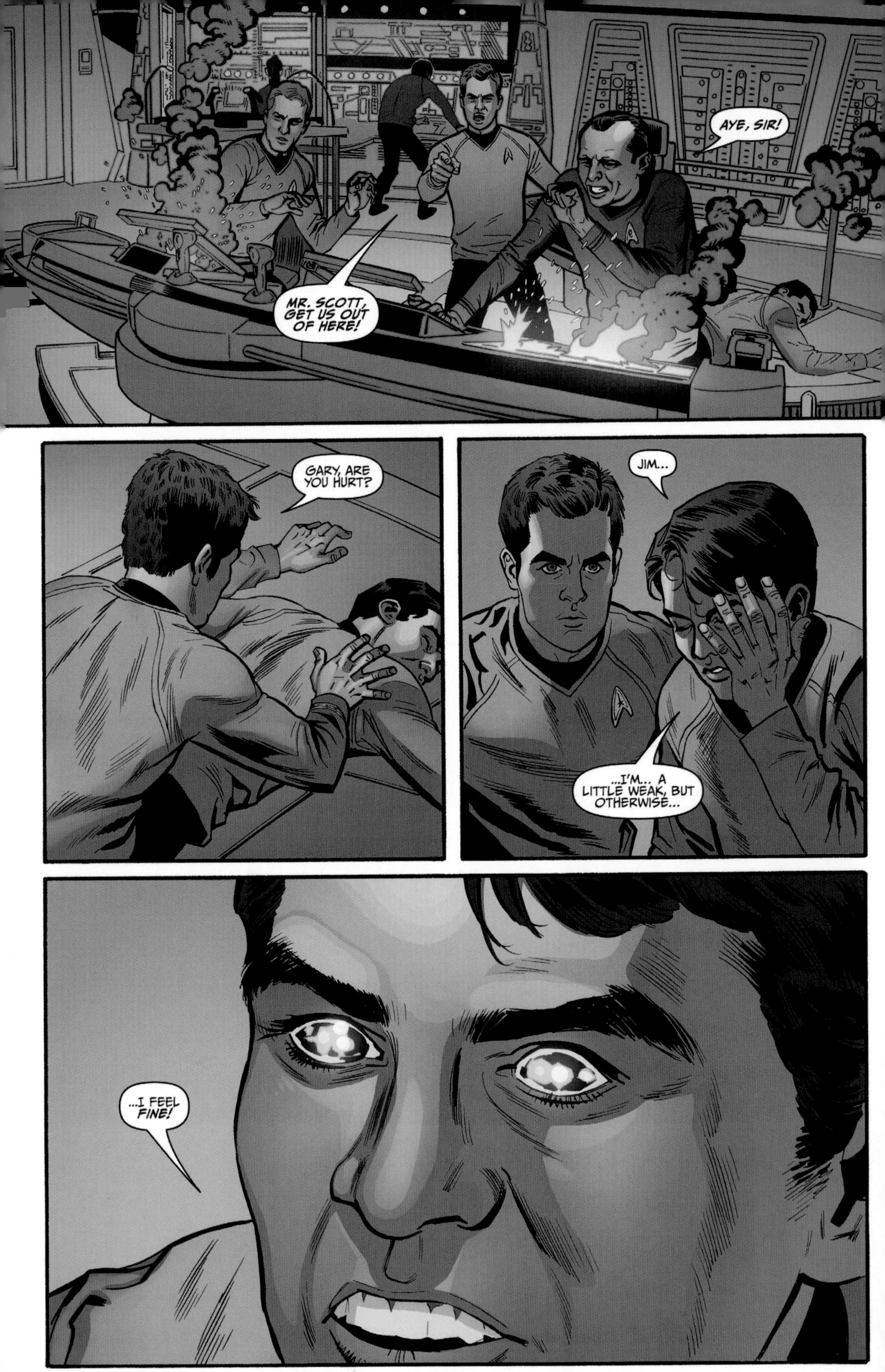
AYE, SIR!
MR. SCOTT, GET US OUT OF HERE!
GARY, ARE YOU HURT?
JIM...
...I'M... A LITTLE WEAK, BUT OTHERWISE...
...I FEEL FINE!

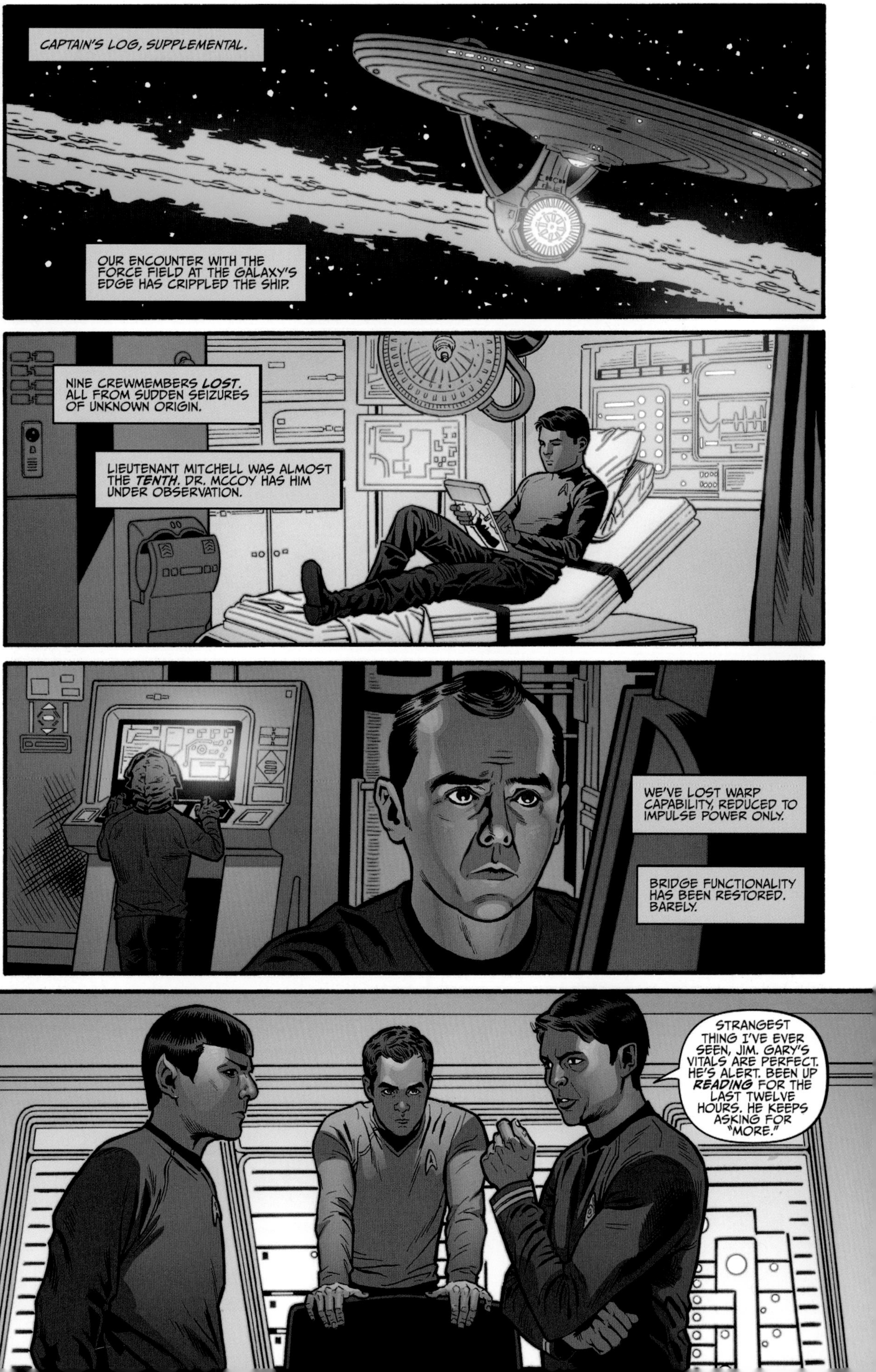
CAPTAIN'S LOG, SUPPLEMENTAL.
OUR ENCOUNTER WITH THE FORCE FIELD AT THE GALAXY'S EDGE HAS CRIPPLED THE SHIP.
NINE CREWMEMBERS *LOST*. ALL FROM SUDDEN SEIZURES OF UNKNOWN ORIGIN.
LIEUTENANT MITCHELL WAS ALMOST THE *TENTH*. DR. MCCOY HAS HIM UNDER OBSERVATION.
WE'VE LOST WARP CAPABILITY, REDUCED TO IMPULSE POWER ONLY.
BRIDGE FUNCTIONALITY HAS BEEN RESTORED. BARELY.
STRANGEST THING I'VE EVER SEEN, JIM. GARY'S VITALS ARE PERFECT. HE'S ALERT. BEEN UP *READING* FOR THE LAST TWELVE HOURS. HE KEEPS ASKING FOR "MORE."

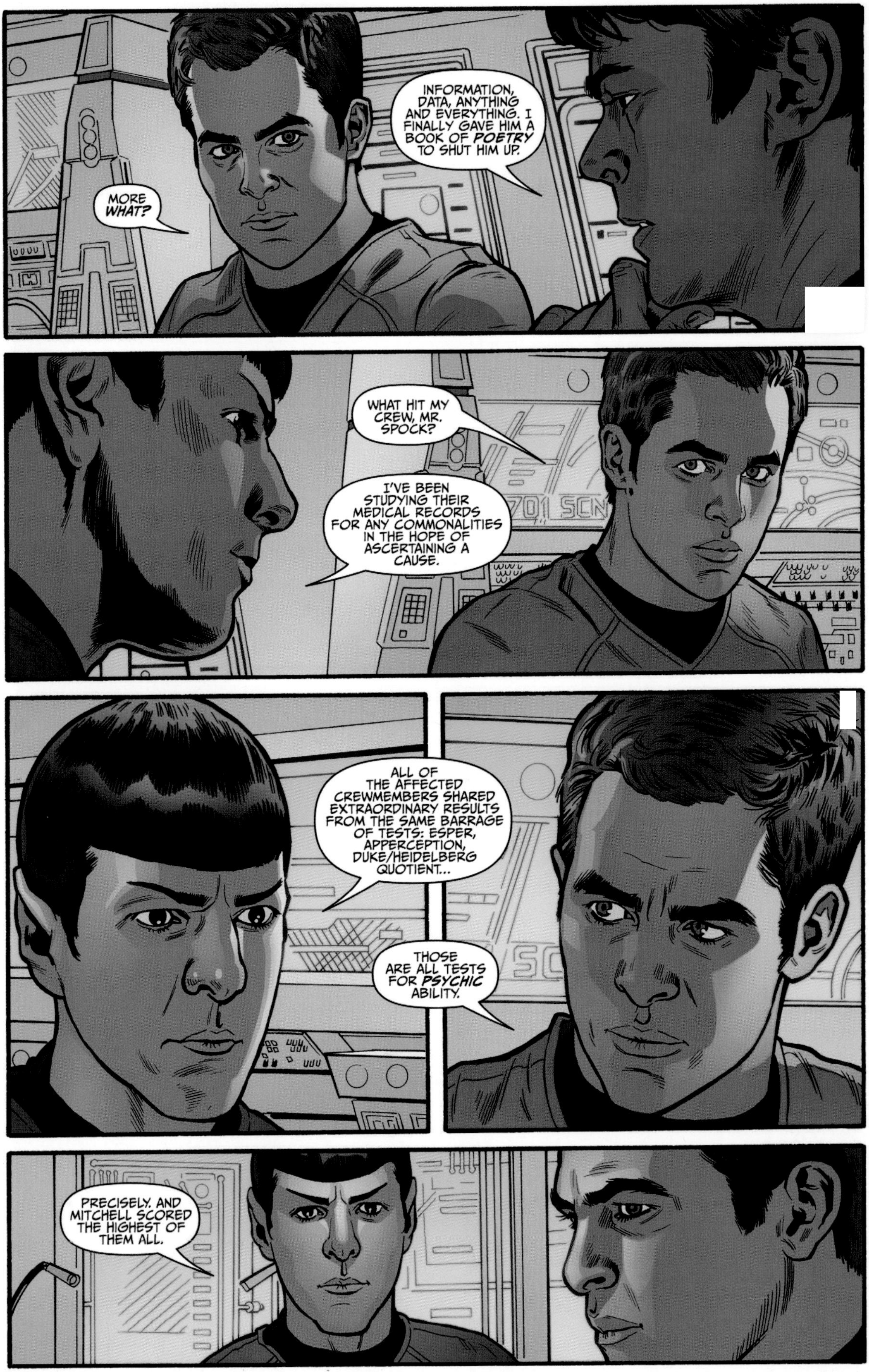
MORE WHAT?
INFORMATION, DATA, ANYTHING AND EVERYTHING. I FINALLY GAVE HIM A BOOK OF POETRY TO SHUT HIM UP.
WHAT HIT MY CREW, MR. SPOCK?
I'VE BEEN STUDYING THEIR MEDICAL RECORDS FOR ANY COMMONALITIES IN THE HOPE OF ASCERTAINING A CAUSE.
ALL OF THE AFFECTED CREWMEMBERS SHARED EXTRAORDINARY RESULTS FROM THE SAME BARRAGE OF TESTS: ESPER, APPERCEPTION, DUKE/HEIDELBERG QUOTIENT...
THOSE ARE ALL TESTS FOR PSYCHIC ABILITY.
PRECISELY. AND MITCHELL SCORED THE HIGHEST OF THEM ALL.

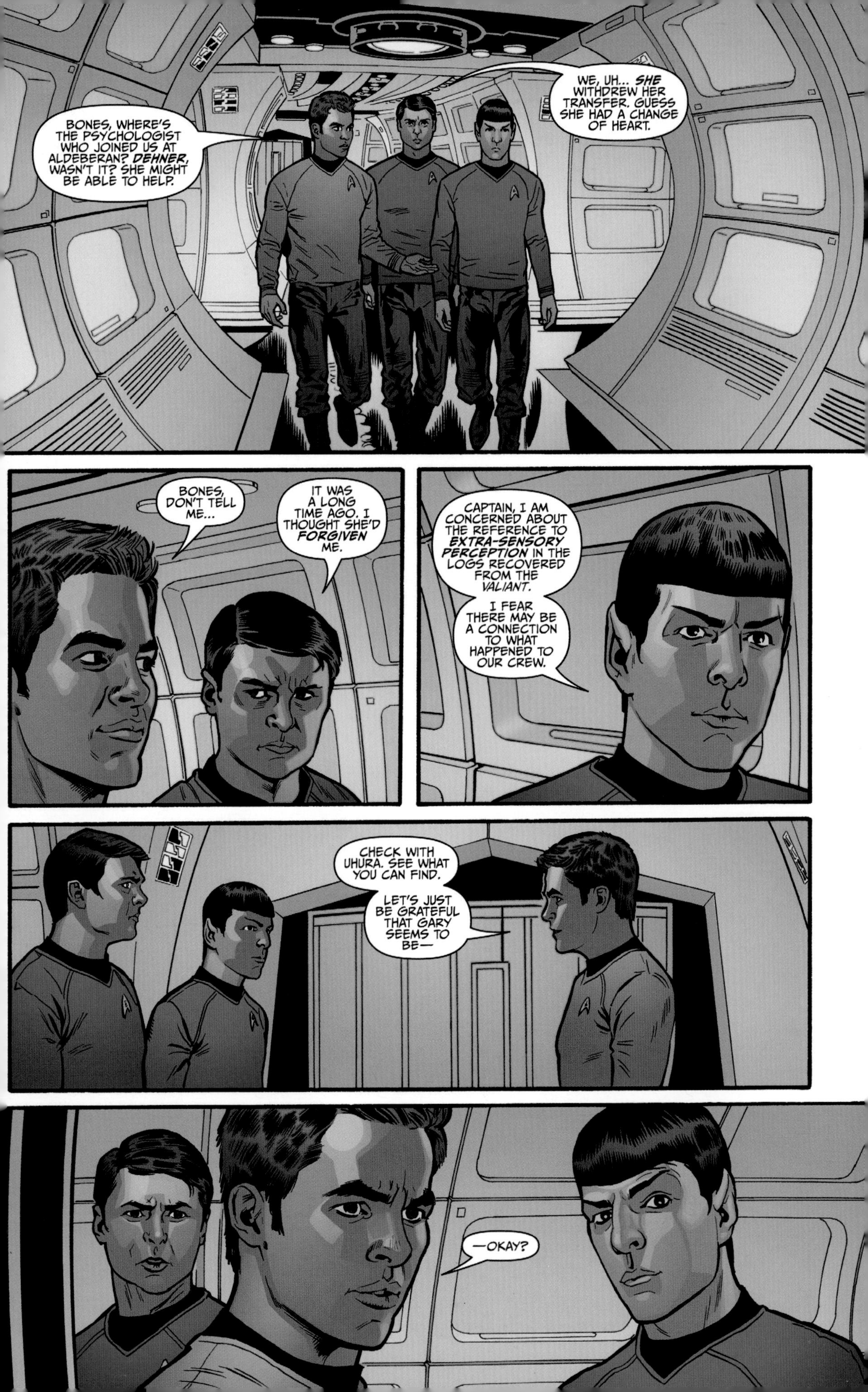
BONES, WHERE'S THE PSYCHOLOGIST WHO JOINED US AT ALDEBERAN? DEHNER, WASN'T IT? SHE MIGHT BE ABLE TO HELP.
WE, UH... SHE WITHDREW HER TRANSFER. GUESS SHE HAD A CHANGE OF HEART.
BONES, DON'T TELL ME...
IT WAS A LONG TIME AGO. I THOUGHT SHE'D FORGIVEN ME.
CAPTAIN, I AM CONCERNED ABOUT THE REFERENCE TO EXTRA-SENSORY PERCEPTION IN THE LOGS RECOVERED FROM THE VALIANT.
I FEAR THERE MAY BE A CONNECTION TO WHAT HAPPENED TO OUR CREW.
CHECK WITH UHURA. SEE WHAT YOU CAN FIND.
LET'S JUST BE GRATEFUL THAT GARY SEEMS TO BE—
—OKAY?

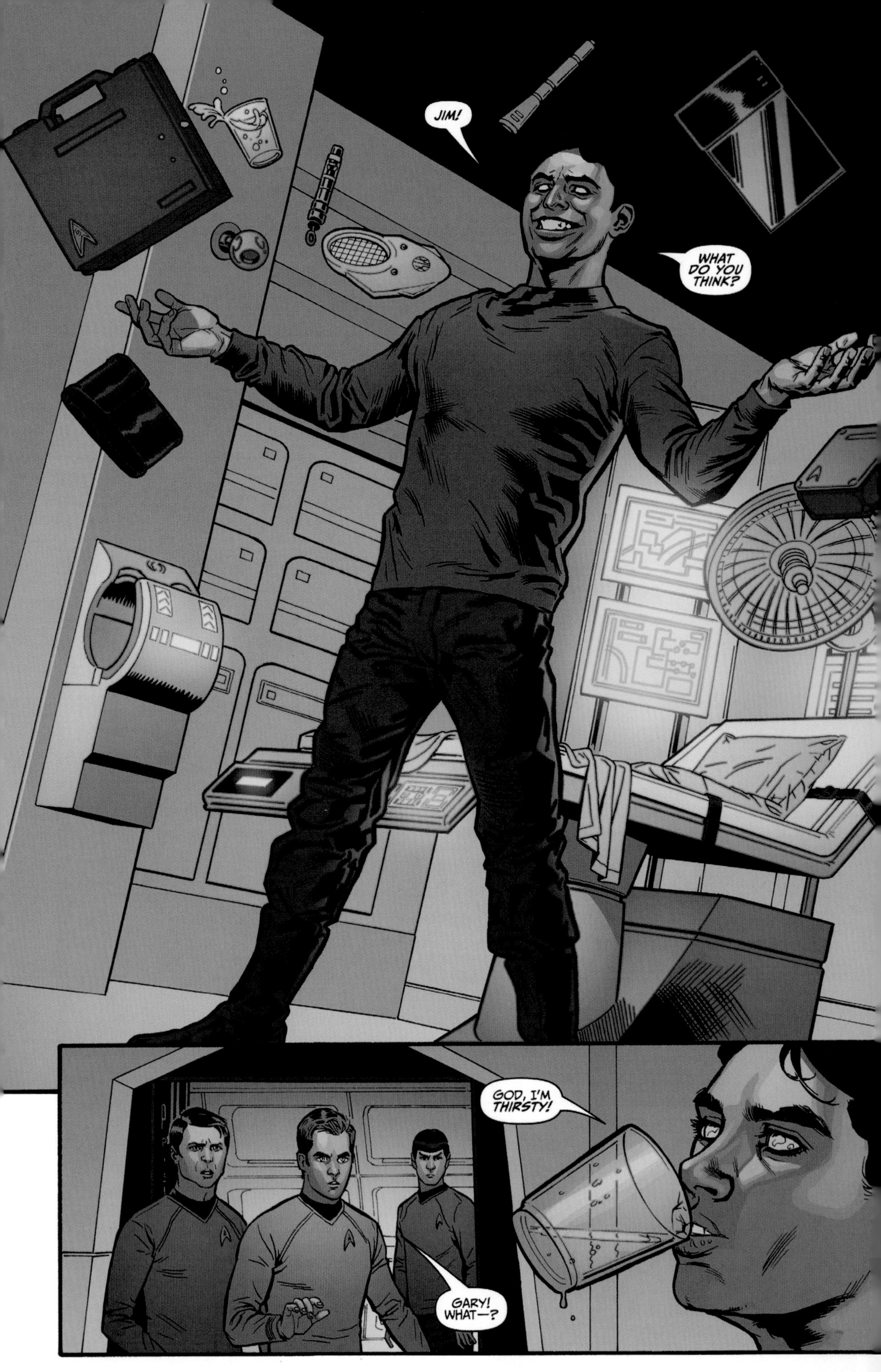
JIM!
WHAT DO YOU THINK?
GOD, I'M THIRSTY!
GARY! WHAT—?

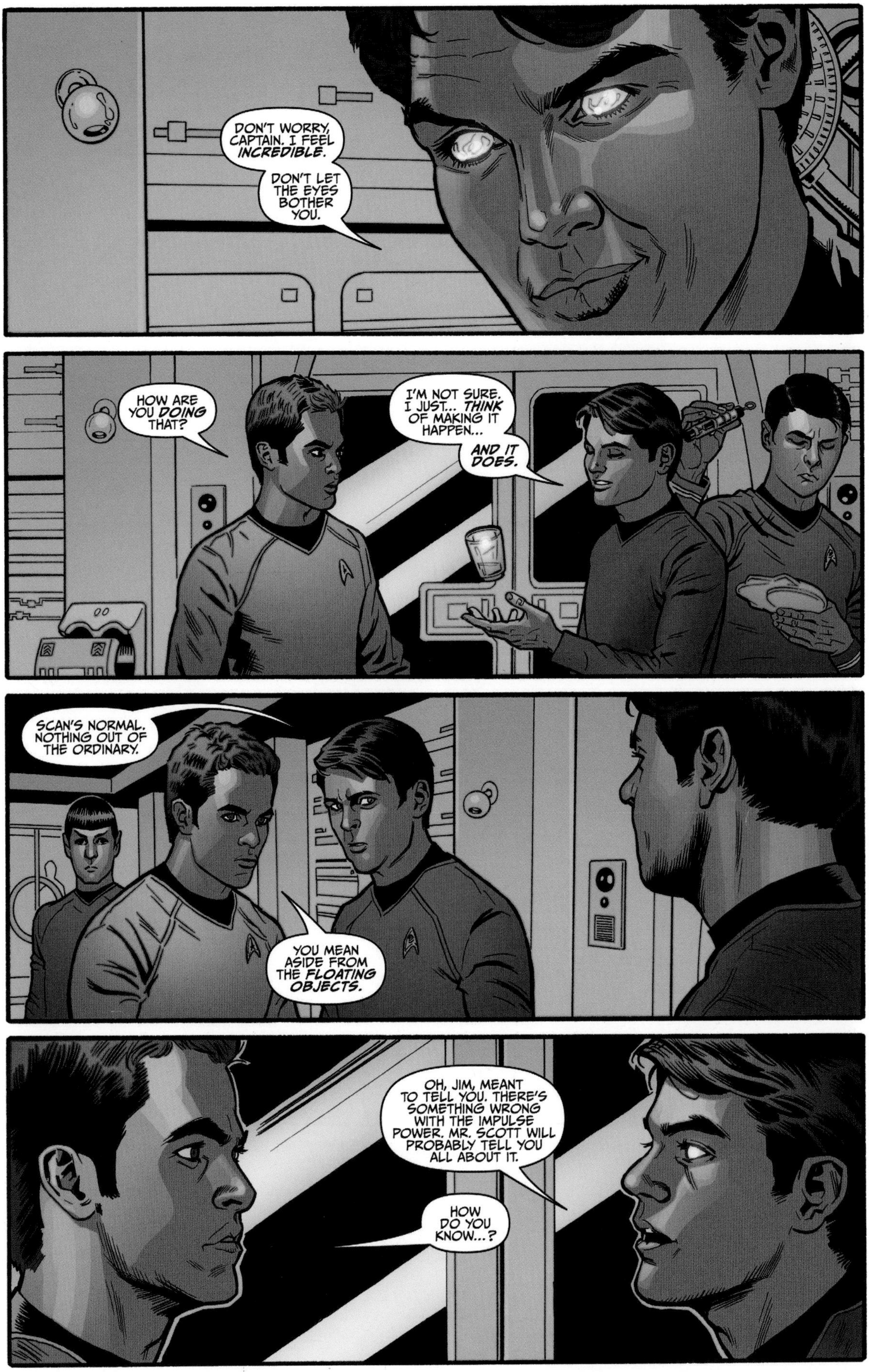
DON'T WORRY, CAPTAIN. I FEEL INCREDIBLE.
DON'T LET THE EYES BOTHER YOU.
HOW ARE YOU DOING THAT?
I'M NOT SURE. I JUST... THINK OF MAKING IT HAPPEN...
AND IT DOES.
SCAN'S NORMAL. NOTHING OUT OF THE ORDINARY.
YOU MEAN ASIDE FROM THE FLOATING OBJECTS.
OH, JIM, MEANT TO TELL YOU. THERE'S SOMETHING WRONG WITH THE IMPULSE POWER. MR. SCOTT WILL PROBABLY TELL YOU ALL ABOUT IT.
HOW DO YOU KNOW...?

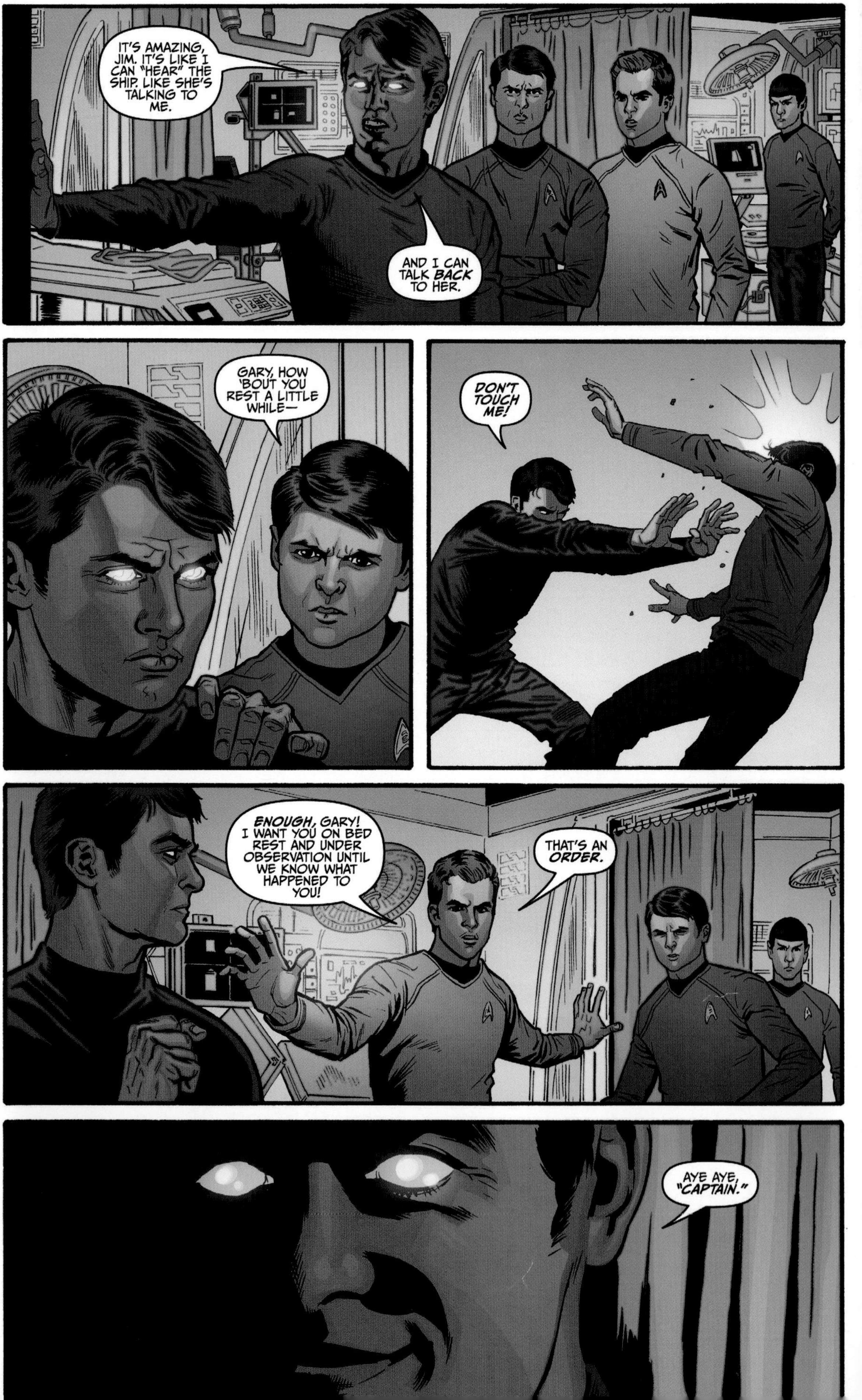
IT'S AMAZING, JIM. IT'S LIKE I CAN "HEAR" THE SHIP. LIKE SHE'S TALKING TO ME.
AND I CAN TALK BACK TO HER.
GARY, HOW 'BOUT YOU REST A LITTLE WHILE—
DON'T TOUCH ME!
ENOUGH, GARY! I WANT YOU ON BED REST AND UNDER OBSERVATION UNTIL WE KNOW WHAT HAPPENED TO YOU!
THAT'S AN ORDER.
AYE AYE, "CAPTAIN."

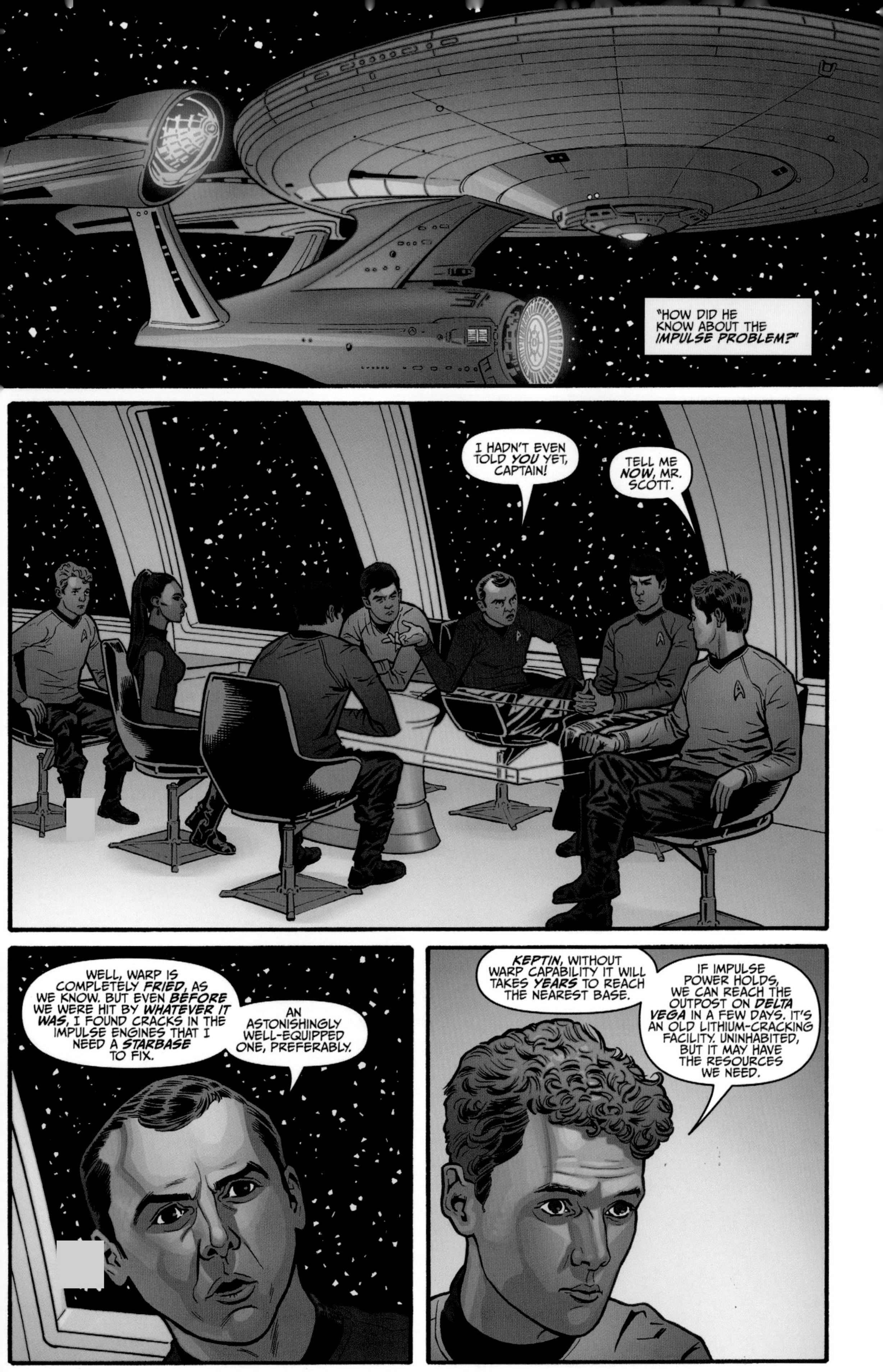
"HOW DID HE KNOW ABOUT THE IMPULSE PROBLEM?"
I HADN'T EVEN TOLD YOU YET, CAPTAIN!
TELL ME NOW, MR. SCOTT.
WELL, WARP IS COMPLETELY FRIED, AS WE KNOW. BUT EVEN BEFORE WE WERE HIT BY WHATEVER IT WAS, I FOUND CRACKS IN THE IMPULSE ENGINES THAT I NEED A STARBASE TO FIX.
AN ASTONISHINGLY WELL-EQUIPPED ONE, PREFERABLY.
KEPTIN, WITHOUT WARP CAPABILITY IT WILL TAKES YEARS TO REACH THE NEAREST BASE.
IF IMPULSE POWER HOLDS, WE CAN REACH THE OUTPOST ON DELTA VEGA IN A FEW DAYS. IT'S AN OLD LITHIUM-CRACKING FACILITY. UNINHABITED, BUT IT MAY HAVE THE RESOURCES WE NEED.

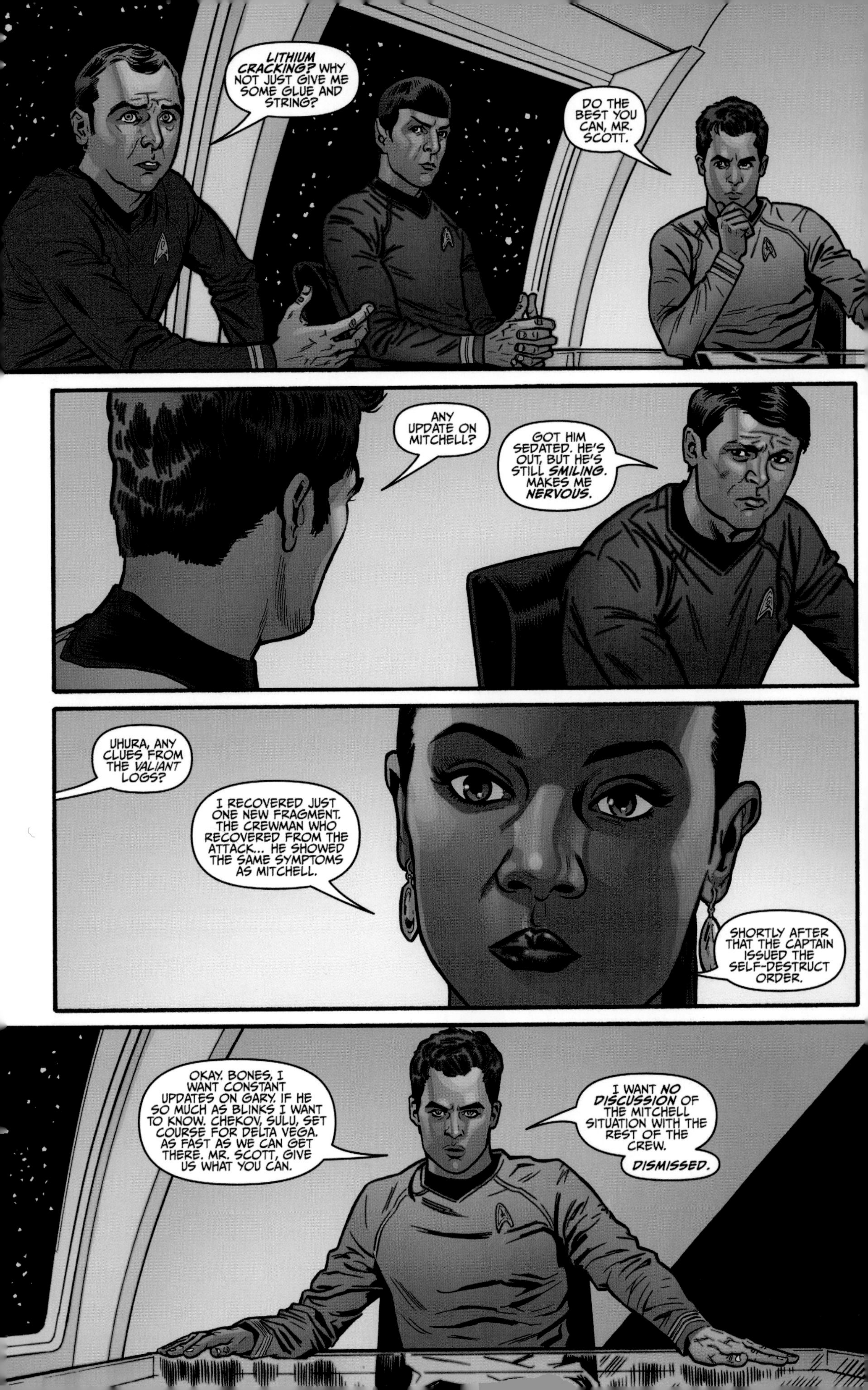
LITHIUM CRACKING? WHY NOT JUST GIVE ME SOME GLUE AND STRING?
DO THE BEST YOU CAN, MR. SCOTT.
ANY UPDATE ON MITCHELL?
GOT HIM SEDATED. HE'S OUT, BUT HE'S STILL SMILING. MAKES ME NERVOUS.
UHURA, ANY CLUES FROM THE VALIANT LOGS?
I RECOVERED JUST ONE NEW FRAGMENT. THE CREWMAN WHO RECOVERED FROM THE ATTACK... HE SHOWED THE SAME SYMPTOMS AS MITCHELL.
SHORTLY AFTER THAT THE CAPTAIN ISSUED THE SELF-DESTRUCT ORDER.
OKAY. BONES, I WANT CONSTANT UPDATES ON GARY. IF HE SO MUCH AS BLINKS I WANT TO KNOW. CHEKOV, SULU, SET COURSE FOR DELTA VEGA. AS FAST AS WE CAN GET THERE. MR. SCOTT, GIVE US WHAT YOU CAN.
I WANT NO DISCUSSION OF THE MITCHELL SITUATION WITH THE REST OF THE CREW.
DISMISSED.

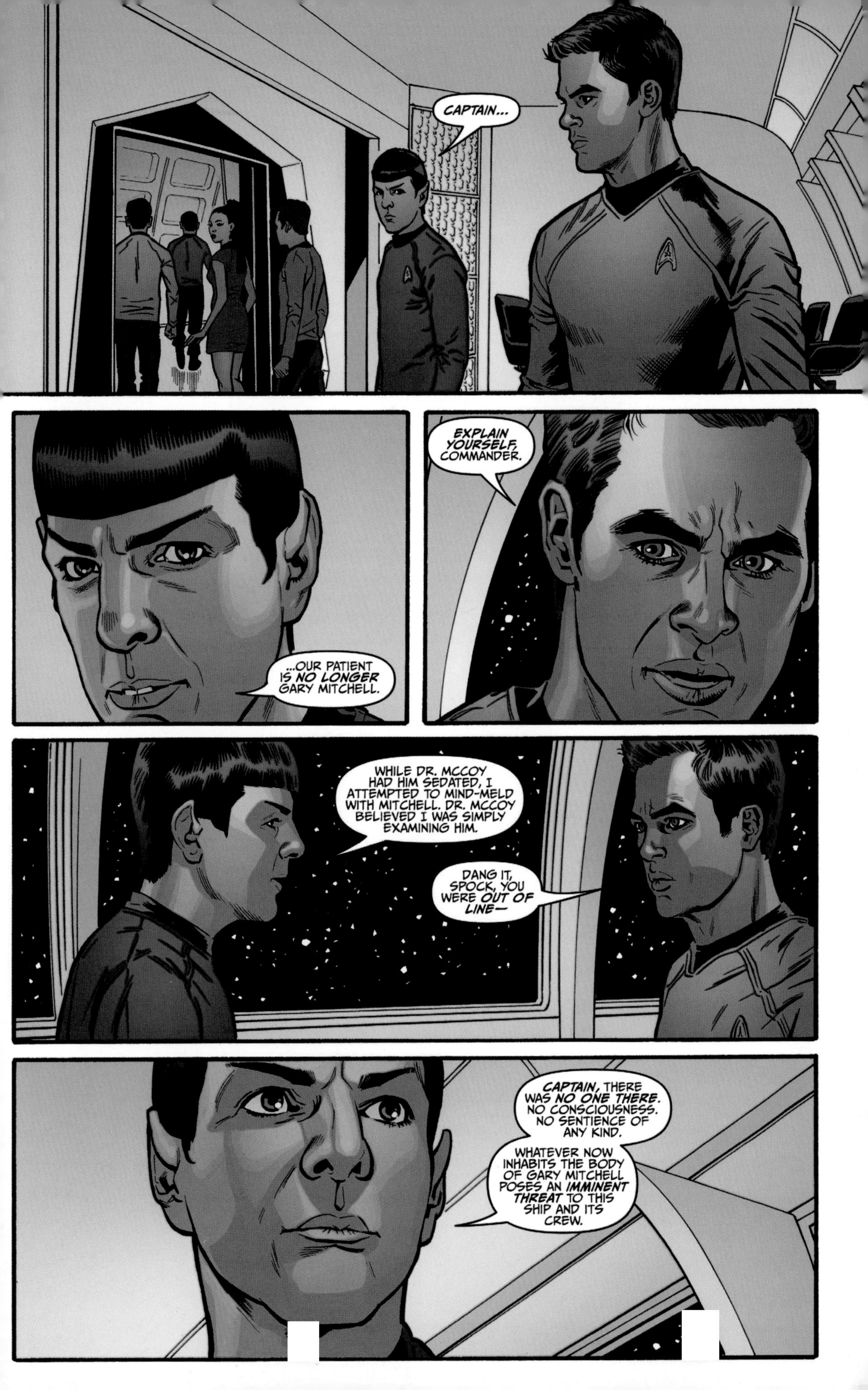
CAPTAIN...
EXPLAIN YOURSELF, COMMANDER.
...OUR PATIENT IS NO LONGER GARY MITCHELL.
WHILE DR. MCCOY HAD HIM SEDATED, I ATTEMPTED TO MIND-MELD WITH MITCHELL. DR. MCCOY BELIEVED I WAS SIMPLY EXAMINING HIM.
DANG IT, SPOCK, YOU WERE OUT OF LINE—
CAPTAIN, THERE WAS NO ONE THERE. NO CONSCIOUSNESS. NO SENTIENCE OF ANY KIND.
WHATEVER NOW INHABITS THE BODY OF GARY MITCHELL POSES AN IMMINENT THREAT TO THIS SHIP AND ITS CREW.

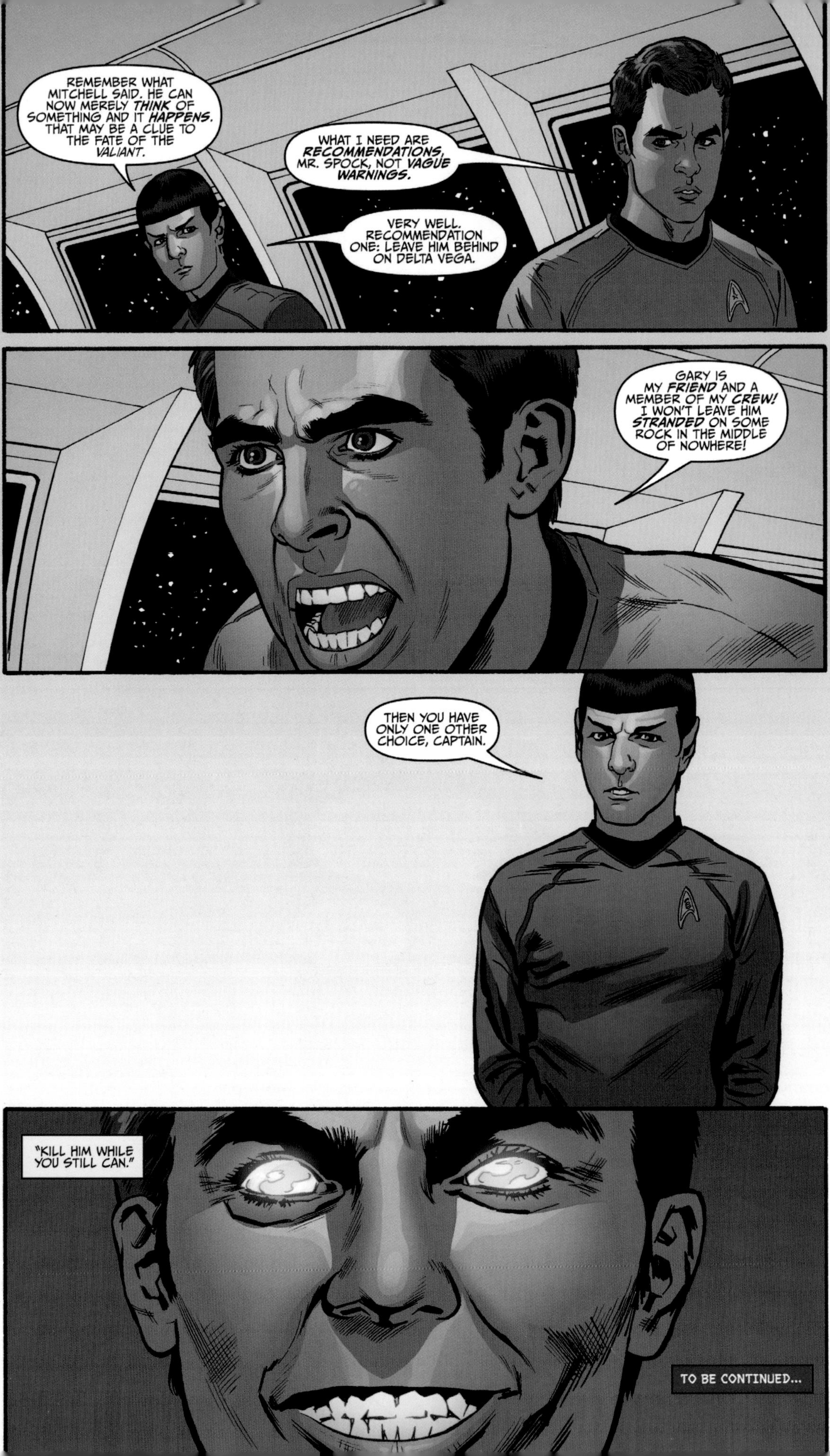
REMEMBER WHAT MITCHELL SAID. HE CAN NOW MERELY *THINK* OF SOMETHING AND IT *HAPPENS*. THAT MAY BE A CLUE TO THE FATE OF THE *VALIANT*.
WHAT I NEED ARE ***RECOMMENDATIONS,*** MR. SPOCK, NOT ***VAGUE WARNINGS.***
VERY WELL. RECOMMENDATION ONE: LEAVE HIM BEHIND ON DELTA VEGA.
GARY IS MY ***FRIEND*** AND A MEMBER OF MY ***CREW!*** I WON'T LEAVE HIM ***STRANDED*** ON SOME ROCK IN THE MIDDLE OF NOWHERE!
THEN YOU HAVE ONLY ONE OTHER CHOICE, CAPTAIN.
"KILL HIM WHILE YOU STILL CAN."
TO BE CONTINUED...